· HARRIET'S ·
HALLOWEEN CANDY

· HARRIET'S ·
HALLOWEEN CANDY

Nancy Carlson

Carolrhoda Books, Inc. ◆ Minneapolis

for my sister, Tuden, because she taught me to draw,
and for my brother, David, because he withstood
so much teasing and still grew up to be a nice guy!

This book is available in two editions:
Library binding by Carolrhoda Books, Inc.
Soft cover by First Avenue Editions
c/o The Lerner Publishing Group
241 First Avenue North
Minneapolis, MN 55401 U.S.A.
Website address: www.lernerbooks.com

LIBRARY OF CONGRESS CATALOGING IN PUBLICATION DATA

Carlson, Nancy L.
  Harriet's Halloween candy.

  Summary: Harriet learns the hard way that
sharing her Halloween candy makes her feel
much better than eating it all herself.
  [1. Halloween — Fiction. 2. Sharing —
Fiction. 3. Confectionary — Fiction. 4. Dogs —
Fiction] I. Title.
PZ7.C21665Har   [E]   81-18140
ISBN 0-87614-182-3 (lib. bdg.)
ISBN 0-87614-850-X (pbk.)

Manufactured in the United States of America
      13 14 15 16 – JP – 02 01 00 99

Harriet really got a lot of candy on Halloween.

When she got home, she laid it all out carefully on the floor. Then she organized it. First by color. Then by size. And finally by favorites.

Harriet's little brother Walter watched. He
was too little to go trick-or-treating.

"Harriet, you be sure you share your candy
with Walt," said Harriet's mother.

"No!" said Harriet. "It's all mine."

But Harriet felt a little guilty.

"Oh, all right," she said. She reached into her
bag and pulled out a teensy-weensy piece of
coconut candy.

Harriet didn't like coconut anyway.

Before Harriet went to bed, she packed her candy in a big box.

Then she hid the box in her closet.

The next morning she got up early to eat
some of her candy.

After she finished three caramel-chocolate bars, she hid the rest behind her bookcase.

Throughout the day Harriet checked on her
candy.

She counted it.

Then she hid it in a new place every time.

Pretty soon Harriet was running out of places to hide it.

"There's only one thing to do," said Harriet.
"I'll have to eat it all up."

So she started to eat. First chocolate bars with peanuts.

Then licorice whips. Then peanut-butter cups.

Then red, blue, green, and orange gumdrops.

"Burp," she said when she got to the saltwater taffy. "I don't feel so good."

"Maybe it's time to share."

"Wouldn't you like a sugar doughnut, Walt?"

"How about some caramel apples?"

"I'm so proud of you, Harriet," said Mother.
"Sharing is a sign of a grown-up dog."

"Oh," said Harriet, "I was going to share all the time."

"That's good, Harriet," said Mother. "Now go wash up for dinner."